The Mystery of the
Wrong Dog

THE THREE COUSINS
DETECTIVE CLUB

———————

#1 / The Mystery of the White Elephant

#2 / The Mystery of the Silent Nightingale

#3 / The Mystery of the Wrong Dog

#4 / The Mystery of the Dancing Angels

#5 / The Mystery of the Hobo's Message

#6 / The Mystery of the Magi's Treasure

#7 / The Mystery of the Haunted Lighthouse

#8 / The Mystery of the Dolphin Detective

#9 / The Mystery of the Eagle Feather

The Mystery of the Wrong Dog

Elspeth Campbell Murphy
Illustrated by Joe Nordstrom

BETHANY HOUSE PUBLISHERS
MINNEAPOLIS, MINNESOTA 55438

Cover and story illustrations by Joe Nordstrom

Published by Bethany House Publishers
A Ministry of Bethany Fellowship, Inc.
11300 Hampshire Avenue South
Minneapolis, Minnesota 55438

Printed in the United States of America

Library of Congress Cataloging-in-Publication Data

Murphy, Elspeth Campbell.
    The mystery of the wrong dog / Elspeth Campbell Murphy.
       p.   cm. — (The Three Cousins Detective Club™ ; 3)
    Summary: Titus and his cousins are taking care of their
neighbors' crabby Yorkshire terrier when the dog suddenly becomes
sweet-tempered and the cousins have a mystery on their hands.

    [1. Mystery and detective stories. 2. Dogs—Fiction.
3. Cousins—Fiction. 4. Christian life—Fiction.] I.Title.
II. Series: Murphy, Elspeth Campbell. Three Cousins Detective
Club™ ; 3.
PZ7.M95315Myr   1994
[Fic]—dc20   94–16716
ISBN 1–55661–407–1   CIP
                                        AC

In loving memory of my father-in-law,

Howard R. Murphy,

whose life was filled with
love, joy, peace,
patience, kindness, goodness,
faithfulness, gentleness, and self-control.

ELSPETH CAMPBELL MURPHY has been a familiar name in Christian publishing for over fifteen years, with more than seventy-five books to her credit and sales reaching five million worldwide. She is the author of the best-selling series *David and I Talk to God* and *The Kids From Apple Street Church,* as well as the 1990 Gold Medallion winner *Do You See Me, God?* A graduate of Trinity College and Moody Bible Institute, Elspeth and her husband, Mike, make their home in Chicago, where she writes full time.

Contents

1. A Peculiar Feeling 9
2. Saint Francis of Assisi 12
3. Crabby Old Kingsley 15
4. At the Bakery 17
5. The Sweetest Dog 22
6. An Emergency Meeting 25
7. Questions 28
8. "The Curious Incident of the Dog
   in the Night-time" 31
9. A Face at the Window 34
10. Doggy Doubles 37
11. *Now* What Do We Do? 41
12. Peacemaking 45
13. Gubbio 50
14. Saint Francis and the Wolf............ 52
15. Home 57

1

A Peculiar Feeling

*T*itus McKay couldn't shake the feeling that he was being watched.

It happened lately whenever he took his neighbor's dog—a scrappy little Yorkshire terrier named Kingsley—for a walk.

Today, even Kingsley seemed to notice that there was something odd. He stopped growling at small children long enough to lift his head and sniff the air.

"Woof?!" he said to Titus, as if demanding an explanation.

"I don't know, boy," Titus said. "It's strange, isn't it?"

The really strange part was that Titus didn't feel afraid. A little uneasy maybe. And definitely puzzled. But not scared.

Titus was a city kid, and he prided himself

on being as streetwise as the next guy. He knew how to play it safe and how to stay alert. Some inner sense told him that he was being watched. But at the same time, he didn't sense danger.

Titus shook his head. "I don't know, Kingsley. It's a peculiar feeling. But we have to go home now anyway. My cousins are coming for a visit. The girl is called Sarah-Jane Cooper. And the boy is called Timothy Dawson. You'll like them."

Actually, Titus doubted that. Kingsley didn't like anybody.

Kingsley belonged to Titus's elderly neighbors, Sam and George. They were two brothers who shared an apartment down the hall from Titus. That is, they *used* to share an apartment until a few days ago when George moved out.

Sam and George were always bickering about one thing or another. But this time George had stomped off to live with his sister, Marie, a few blocks away. Then Sam had gone into the hospital.

So Kingsley had moved in with Titus for a while.

For Titus, having Kingsley live in his own apartment was a kind of test to prove how well he could handle a dog of his own.

More than anything else in the world, Titus wanted a dog of his own. His parents were just about convinced. The way Titus saw it, saying they would think about it was just one small step away from saying yes.

Titus was good with animals. He held a job in his building feeding fish and birds and cats when the owners were away. He was also a good dog walker. That's how he had gotten to know Kingsley in the first place.

Kingsley. What a dog. Titus called him "good dog" whenever he could. But that was stretching things a bit. Kingsley was never actually "good." But with Titus he was "less bad" most of the time. Titus was just about the only person besides Sam and George who could handle him. Titus's father said that was because Kingsley thought Titus was the "top dog," the "leader of the pack."

And Titus had pointed out that if he could handle Kingsley, he could certainly handle a dog of his own.

His parents were just about convinced.

2

Saint Francis of Assisi

At the side of Titus's building there was a peaceful little courtyard. At the center of the courtyard, there was a gently splashing fountain. It was called the Saint Francis fountain. On the edge of the fountain stood a statue of a man in a long robe. He was Saint Francis of Assisi. And Titus thought he had one of the nicest faces he had ever seen. Carved birds sat peacefully on his shoulders, and small animals gathered at his feet.

Titus was good with animals. But he wasn't *that* good. No one he knew could get wild animals to come close like that.

Most amazing of all was that Saint Francis's hand rested on the head of a big wolf. Not a big dog. A wolf. Not everyone could tell the difference between, say, an Alaskan malamute or a Siberian husky and a wolf. But Titus could. And this was a wolf. Titus was sure of it. But what it was doing there with Saint Francis, he had no idea.

Around the edge of the basin were carved the words: *Lord, make me an instrument of Thy peace.*

Whenever Titus passed the fountain, he wondered about those words. Although, if Kingsley was with him, he didn't have much time to wonder about anything.

Kingsley seemed to think it was his job to clear the courtyard of every living thing—except himself. He dashed about, barking his little head off. Pigeons rose in a noisy flapping of wings. Sparrows scattered, chattering, to the streetlights. Squirrels dashed to the nearest trees.

"Kingsley, you are the most UNpeaceful animal on the face of the earth," Titus scolded. "Do you notice that not even Saint Francis of Assisi has a Yorkshire terrier? He'd rather have a wolf."

Kingsley muttered something under his breath that Titus couldn't quite catch and headed for the building.

But just at that moment, the side door burst open, and Timothy and Sarah-Jane tumbled out.

"We got here early, Ti," Timothy said. "Aunt Jane said you were out walking the dog, so we came to meet you."

"Oh, look at the sweet little dog!" cried Sarah-Jane. "Oh, Ti! He's so cute I can't stand it!"

And before Titus could stop her, Sarah-Jane reached out to cuddle Kingsley.

3

Crabby Old Kingsley

*S*arah-Jane screamed and jumped back.

"What happened?" cried Timothy. "Did he bite you?"

Sarah-Jane shook her head.

"Scared you, though," said Titus.

Sarah-Jane nodded.

To give Kingsley credit, he never actually bit anyone. But he was always threatening to. And that was almost as bad.

"Bad dog!" said Titus sternly. "Bad, bad, bad, bad dog. Sarah-Jane was just trying to be nice to you. Why do you have to go and embarrass me in front of my cousins? Now, *be good.*"

In all the commotion, Titus had dropped the leash. Timothy picked it up. Kingsley twisted around and got his end of the leash in his mouth. He jerked the leash right out of Timothy's hand.

"Ow!" yelled Timothy. But it was so funny he and Titus started to laugh. "That dog is a menace to society," added Timothy cheerfully.

But Sarah-Jane wasn't quite over her hurt feelings yet. "It's not fair! Dogs that horrible shouldn't be allowed to look so cute. How's a person supposed to know you can't pick them up and cuddle them?"

By now Titus had a firm hold on the leash and had even gotten Kingsley to heel.

"Don't tell on him, OK, you guys?" Titus pleaded. "I'm trying to prove to my mom and dad that I can handle a dog of my own. And they might change their minds if they find out how bad Kingsley was today. I don't want to take any chances."

Timothy said, "What are the chances any other dog would be that crabby?"

"Crabby old Kingsley," muttered Sarah-Jane.

"Woof!" said Kingsley.

"Who asked you?" said Sarah-Jane.

But Kingsley hadn't actually done any harm. So both Sarah-Jane and Timothy promised not to tell on him.

4

At the Bakery

"*O*h, I almost forgot," said Timothy. "Your mom gave us some money. She said you should take us to Petersen's Bakery. She said we can pick out whatever we want for dessert tonight."

"Oh, wow," said Titus. "You guys are not going to believe this place. It has the most EXcellent stuff."

They set off for the bakery with Kingsley. He behaved pretty well except for putting up a little bit of a fuss when they came to a busy intersection and Titus picked him up.

Titus explained, "His owners, Sam and George, say it's safer this way. You don't have much time to get across. Besides, Kingsley is so short, his face is close to the car exhaust

17

pipes. It's not good for you to breathe in all those fumes, is it, boy?"

Kingsley couldn't really argue with that. So he stopped fussing, and they hurried across the street.

In all that had happened, the feeling never left Titus that he was being watched.

He put Kingsley down on the other side of the street and told his cousins about it.

Timothy and Sarah-Jane were fascinated. They loved mysteries, and so did Titus. In fact, the three of them even had a club called the Three Cousins Detective Club. They had solved quite a few mysteries. But they didn't know what to make of this one.

"Do you feel like you're being watched, too?" asked Titus.

"Yes, now that you mention it," said Sarah-Jane. "But maybe it's just my imagination *because* you mentioned it."

Timothy stopped and sniffed the air, much as Kingsley had done earlier. He said, "I don't think we're imagining things. Something's odd. But I don't know what."

They were almost at the bakery. And when they got there, one look in the window made it

18

hard to think of anything but dessert.

"Neat-O!" said Timothy.

"So cool!" agreed Sarah-Jane.

"Didn't I tell you it was EXcellent?" asked Titus, feeling very pleased.

Dogs weren't allowed in the store, of course. But that was all right. City dogs were used to waiting patiently out on the sidewalk while their owners shopped. Even Kingsley.

Titus tied Kingsley's leash to a "No Parking" sign and told him to be good. Fortunately, there were no other dogs that day for Kingsley to argue with.

The three cousins stepped into the bakery and just about passed out from all the delicious smells.

It took a while to pick out what they wanted. But finally they came out with a pink cardboard box tied up with string.

Kingsley did a little doggy dance of joy when they came over to him.

"What's gotten into Kingsley?" asked Timothy. "Does he want dessert?"

"He never has before," said Titus. "I tried giving him a piece of cake once. But he wouldn't eat it."

"Well, something sure put him in a good mood," said Timothy. "Let me try taking the leash again."

This time Kingsley didn't jerk the leash out of Timothy's hand. Instead, he trotted along contentedly with no complaints at all.

When they got to the intersection, Titus went to pick him up. But Sarah-Jane's arms were aching for the feel of fur. So she said bravely, "Let me try."

Kingsley didn't squirm and he didn't fuss. Instead he nestled down peacefully in Sarah-Jane's arms, to her great delight.

20

She said, "You just needed time to get used to us, didn't you, Kingsley? Oh, you're just the sweetest, cutest, cuddliest little dog in the whole world!"

"S-J!" wailed Titus. "That's enough to make anyone want to bite you."

But Kingsley didn't bite. He didn't even threaten to. He just looked at them all with eyes full of love and licked Sarah-Jane on the chin.

Titus was so puzzled by all of this that it took him a while to notice something else.

The feeling of being watched was completely gone.

5

The Sweetest Dog

Dogs weren't allowed in the people elevator. So the cousins and Kingsley went in the back way and rode the freight elevator to the nineteenth floor.

They walked down the hall. That is, the cousins walked. Kingsley was still getting a free ride. Sarah-Jane hadn't wanted to set him down after she'd carried him across the intersection. So she had carried him all the way home. And—to Titus's surprise—Kingsley had seemed to enjoy every minute of it.

They passed Sam and George's apartment. At least, it *used* to belong to both of them—until the big argument when George had moved out.

Usually Titus had a hard time with Kingsley at this spot. Kingsley would whine and paw at the door, wanting to go home to his two owners. And Titus couldn't really blame him. Homesick was a lousy feeling.

But today Kingsley just ignored his own apartment and went happily to Titus's at the end of the hall.

When the cousins and Kingsley came in, Titus's father looked up from the super-duper spaghetti sauce that he was making for dinner.

"Well, I'll be! Looks like you made a friend, Sarah-Jane."

"Oh, Uncle Richard, he's just the *sweetest dog*!"

"Who's the sweetest dog?" asked Titus's mother, coming into the kitchen.

"Kingsley," said Titus's father, waiting to see the astonished look on his wife's face. He was not disappointed.

"*Kingsley!?*" exclaimed Titus's mother. "That dog is more ornery than any cat I ever saw. If we're even a few minutes late with his supper, he kicks his dish across the floor."

"Well, look at him now," her husband replied.

Sarah-Jane's arms were getting tired. Reluctantly she set Kingsley down. He went right to his water dish and got a drink. But—to the McKays' surprise—he didn't sit barking at the cabinet where the dog biscuits were kept. That's what he usually did when he came in from a walk.

Titus got him a dog biscuit anyway. Kingsley seemed delighted, not demanding.

"Good dog!" said Titus. It felt strange to say that to Kingsley and really mean it.

Titus's mother shook her head as if she couldn't quite believe what she was seeing. "Well, I must say, you've done wonders with Kingsley. He's like a different dog."

"Good work, Son," said his father. "I'm really impressed with the way you handle him."

Timothy and Sarah-Jane nudged Titus excitedly. Things were going great. If this kept up, Titus would soon have a dog of his own.

But Titus didn't feel excited. And he didn't feel peaceful about how things were going. Something was seriously out of order. And he knew that until he faced up to it, he wouldn't have any peace.

He called an emergency meeting of the Three Cousins Detective Club.

6

An Emergency Meeting

*I*n his room Titus had a big poster that showed all the different breeds of dog. It was not everyone who knew the difference between a greyhound and a whippet. But Titus did.

Titus used to think that when it came to dogs, bigger was better. He spent hours trying to decide between a Great Dane and an Irish wolfhound. Dogs didn't come any bigger than that. But he knew this was just an imaginary decision. Just like his imaginary way of getting to school in the winter. By dog sled.

But Titus knew that a little dog who was real was better than any big dog who was imaginary. Titus looked over at the little Yorkshire terrier, who was sniffing at the dog bed as if he had never seen it before. And Titus realized with a pang that of all the dogs on his poster, of all the dogs in the world, he wanted *this* dog.

But there was a problem.

Timothy and Sarah-Jane looked expectantly at him, waiting to hear what this emergency meeting was all about.

Titus cleared his throat and got right to the point.

"You guys? This dog isn't Kingsley."

"*What?!*" cried Timothy and Sarah-Jane together.

Titus held up his hand. "No, don't say anything yet. Just listen a minute."

He ticked off the points with his fingers.

"One: Kingsley doesn't like anybody. But when we came out of the bakery, he was delighted to see us.

"Two: When you first saw Kingsley, back in the courtyard, he grabbed the leash out of Tim's hands. But when we came out of the bakery, he let Tim take the leash—no problem.

"Three: When Sarah-Jane first tried to pet Kingsley, he practically scared her to death. When we came out of the bakery, he let her carry him across the intersection. He let her carry him all the way home.

"Four: When we came back, Kingsley

didn't whine at his own apartment. Why? Because this dog has never been here before. It's not his apartment. And he's not Kingsley.

"Five: This dog didn't bark at the cabinet where we keep Kingsley's dog biscuits. Why? Because this dog has never been in my kitchen before. He didn't even know there *were* dog biscuits—let alone where we keep them."

Sarah-Jane and Timothy had listened seriously. But Titus could tell they had some doubts about what he was saying.

Sarah-Jane asked, "But doesn't all that just prove that you know how to handle Kingsley and make him be good? Even your parents said that."

Titus shook his head. "They haven't spent as much time with Kingsley as I have. Believe me, *no* one could make Kingsley be this good. Saint Francis of Assisi couldn't make Kingsley be this good."

"So what you're saying—" began Timothy carefully, "is that someone *switched* dogs with us?"

"That's exactly what I'm saying," replied Titus.

7

Questions

"*T*hat doesn't make sense, Ti," said Sarah-Jane. "Why would anyone switch dogs? Why would anyone want crabby old Kingsley when they could have this dog? He's the sweetest dog in the world."

"S-J!" exclaimed Titus. "Listen to what you just said. You *know* this isn't Kingsley."

Sarah-Jane and Timothy looked again at the Yorkshire terrier, curled up on the floor beside Titus with his chin resting on Titus's ankle. (Was there any cozier feeling in the world?) Suddenly his cousins saw what Titus meant.

Titus stroked the dog's silky fur. "We went to the bakery with Kingsley. And we came back with this little guy." He added softly, sadly, "I don't even know his name."

Titus's mind was whirling with questions,

which he put to his cousins. "Who took Kingsley? Why? Where is he now? And how in the world am I going to get him back?"

Sarah-Jane gave an awkward little cough, as if she were embarrassed to be asking. "Do you absolutely *have* to get Kingsley back? I mean, this little dog is so wonderful. And Kingsley is so—"

"Of course I have to get Kingsley back," Titus moaned. "Sam will know right away that this isn't his dog. How is that going to look? He goes into the hospital. He trusts me with his dog. He comes back and discovers I put another dog in his place. He's going to want to know what I did with Kingsley."

"You didn't do anything with Kingsley," said Sarah-Jane. "Someone took him."

"Who's going to believe that?" asked Titus. "It all sounds so crazy." The questions came rushing back: "Who took Kingsley? Why? Where is he now?"

"I have another question," said Timothy. Gently he picked up the dog and set him on his lap. "See? He's wearing Kingsley's dog tag. That means whoever switched dogs had to switch collars, too. Right? And my question is: How? I can see getting the collar off this little guy. But think of the Kingsley we all know and love. Can you imagine him letting *anyone* get close enough to take his collar off? Why didn't we hear anything? Kingsley would have barked his fool head off."

As soon as Timothy said that, Titus felt as if a light bulb had switched on in his head. Just like in the comics.

He knew who took Kingsley.

He knew why.

And he had a pretty good idea of where Kingsley was.

He jumped up and said, "Listen, you guys! I want to read you something."

8

"The Curious Incident of the Dog in the Night-time"

*H*is cousins stared at him open-mouthed. "You want to *read* us something?" asked Sarah-Jane, as if she couldn't be hearing right. "What about Kingsley?"

"This is about Kingsley," said Titus.

He went to his bookshelf and pulled down a very large, very well-worn book. It was called *The Complete Sherlock Holmes.*

Titus said, "My Grand-uncle Frank gave this book to my dad when he was a kid. Then my dad gave it to me."

The stories were kind of long and hard for Titus to get through on his own. So he and his father had read them together.

Timothy and Sarah-Jane waited patiently while Titus hunted for the page he wanted.

"OK," said Titus. "Here it is. This story is called 'Silver Blaze.' That's the name of this really valuable racehorse that gets stolen. So Sherlock Holmes and his friend Dr. Watson get called out to the farm to see what happened. And the policeman—the inspector—is there, too. And he knows Sherlock Holmes is this great detective. So the inspector asks Sherlock Holmes for advice. OK? Here it is. The inspector says:

" 'Is there any point to which you would wish to draw my attention?'

" 'To the curious incident of the dog in the night-time.' That's Sherlock Holmes talking. Then the inspector says—

" 'The dog did nothing in the night-time.'

" 'That was the curious incident,' remarked Sherlock Holmes."

Timothy said, "The dog did *nothing*? That *is* weird. *Very* curious. A horse gets stolen right out from under his nose, and he doesn't even bark or anything? He's not much of a watchdog if he lets strangers come in and steal like that."

"That's exactly what Sherlock Holmes was getting at," said Titus.

"Unless—" said Sarah-Jane, thinking out loud. "Unless it wasn't a stranger. What if it was an inside job? What if the horse was taken by someone the dog knew? He wouldn't bark then!"

"Bingo!" said Titus. "That's just what happened in the story."

"And that's what you think happened with Kingsley!" said Timothy. "He didn't bark when somebody took him. Because *he was taken by somebody he knew!*"

By this time, Titus was pacing around his small room. It was hard not to trip over the Yorkshire terrier, who was trotting along at his heels.

Titus said, "As far as I know, there are only three people on earth who could have gotten Kingsley's collar off and taken him away—without World War III breaking out. I'm one of them. Sam's in the hospital. So that leaves just one."

9

A Face at the Window

*T*itus's parents had a rule that he always had to tell them where he was going. And if something came up while he was out, he always had to call home.

"Mom, Tim and Sarah-Jane and I are going over to see George at his sister Marie's house, OK?"

"Oh, I think that would be very nice," said his mother. "I'm sure George is lonely without Sam. And I know Sam misses George. I wish those two would patch up their differences and make peace with each other. This building is George's home, after all. He's lived here forever. And Sam is going to need someone around when he comes home from the hospital. You're taking Kingsley, aren't you? I'm sure George would love to see him."

The excitement of Titus's hunch was beginning to wear off for him. In fact, he was beginning to wonder if the "great dog switch" was all his imagination. He didn't want to say any more about it until he had checked it out.

"Uh, right. We're taking the dog. Come on, boy."

It seemed the Yorkie couldn't believe his good luck at getting another walk so soon with his favorite people. Titus had to wait to put the leash on until the terrier had done another little doggy dance of joy.

At the Saint Francis fountain the Yorkie couldn't resist chasing the pigeons for the sheer fun of it. He didn't seem to take the pigeons as seriously as Kingsley had.

Titus led his cousins down some quiet, peaceful side streets, lined with tall, narrow houses. But Titus didn't feel peaceful. His mind kept doing flip-flops. One minute he was positive he was right. The next minute he was sure he was wrong. And if it turned out he was wrong, he knew he was going to feel pretty stupid. But he also knew that sometimes you have to risk feeling stupid if you want to find something out.

When they came to Marie's house, Titus hesitated. He was having one of his "sure-he-was-wrong moments" right then. He glanced at his cousins. Somehow he could sense that Timothy and Sarah-Jane were feeling pretty tense, too. Titus was so glad that he could count on his cousins not to make fun of him if this turned out to be a wild-goose chase.

The three of them stood there, looking up at the house. Suddenly a face appeared at the window. A fierce face.

A fierce, furry, yapping, little face.

The cousins burst out laughing.

Kingsley!

10

Doggy Doubles

*A*s soon as Titus's dog saw Kingsley, he started barking, too.

That made Kingsley bark all the more.

Stereo Yorkies yapping their furry little heads off. Not a pretty sound.

The door opened and George looked out. "Ah, Titus," he said. "I should have known you would catch on. Give me a minute. Let me put Kingsley in the backyard."

The cousins stood waiting on the small front porch. They could hear George leading a furious Kingsley down the hall and out the back door.

Marie bustled to the front door. "George!" she called over her shoulder. "Why did you leave these children standing on the front porch? I'm telling you, that dog of yours will have to go. We can't even have visitors with him around!" To the cousins she said, "Come in, darlings. Come in. Come in."

She led them into a small living room crammed with old-fashioned but beautiful furniture. Titus knew the Yorkie wouldn't chew it. But Titus picked him up and put him on his lap anyway.

Marie was surprised to see another Yorkshire terrier. "Am I seeing double?" she asked. "Now *that* is a nice dog. I told my brother I don't mind having a nice dog. But that other one!" She cocked her head toward the backyard.

The cousins glanced at one another. Kingsley—the real Kingsley—had not exactly made friends with Marie.

Marie said, "I'm a cat person myself. I used to have a cat. But she died."

"Oh, I'm sorry," said Sarah-Jane.

"It's very sweet of you to say so, my dear. My cat was very old. I had her for a long time. I didn't want to get another cat for a while. But then I felt ready to get another kitten. That's when my brother George wanted to move in with his dog. And I thought, 'A cute little dog. How bad could that be?' "

The cousins glanced at one another again. Knowing Kingsley, pretty bad.

Marie said, "I didn't know what Kingsley was like. Whenever I had my brothers over for dinner, they had to leave the dog at home. Because of my cat, you see.

"So anyway, George moves in with his dog. And at first everything was fine. He was the sweetest dog you ever saw. Just like yours. Then my brother took him for a walk today. And the dog comes back mean and crabby. Almost like a different dog. Do you know what he did? Stood barking for a dog biscuit. And when I didn't get it for him right away, he kicked his supper dish across the floor. Have you ever heard of such a thing?"

The cousins glanced at one another yet again. Yes, actually. They had heard of a dog doing that.

Just then George came back. It had taken him a while to get Kingsley calmed down.

Titus realized that in all the fuss with Kingsley, he hadn't introduced his cousins to George and Marie. Everyone said, "How are you?" "Pleased to meet you."

And then Marie asked, "And what's your dog's name, Titus?"

"He's not exactly my dog," said Titus wistfully. "And—I don't know his name."

"His name is Gubbio," said George. "It's spelled G-U-B-B-I-O, and it's pronounced GOO—bee—oh."

Marie was suspicious as she turned to her brother. "How is it you know Titus's dog's name—and Titus doesn't?"

George sighed. "It's a long story."

"Let's hear it," said his sister.

11

Now What Do We Do?

*G*eorge said, "Gubbio belonged to friends of mine who moved overseas. It would have been too complicated to take a dog with them. Much as they hated to give him up! Anyway, they knew I didn't have a dog anymore. And they knew I liked Yorkies. So they asked if I would like to have Gubbio. And I said I would be delighted. It seemed like the perfect arrangement. I even thought if I renamed him Kingsley, it would be like old times. Except— except that I missed the *real* Kingsley."

Marie and the cousins stared at him in disbelief.

Timothy said, "You mean to tell us you had Gubbio, but you missed *Kingsley*?"

"That Kingsley—he doesn't like women," said Marie.

"Tell me about it!" said Sarah-Jane.

"Kingsley doesn't like anybody," said Titus.

"Woof!" said Gubbio.

George didn't argue with them. "I know. I know. Kingsley is a crabby old thing. But then—so am I. And he's my *dog*, you know?"

"Yours and Sam's," Marie corrected him.

George sighed. "I know. You're right, of course. I knew Sam would never give me Kingsley. So I—I took him. I tried to convince myself that I was doing Sam a favor. I told myself I didn't just take Kingsley and leave him without a dog. I told myself it would be *better* for Sam to have a nice, quiet, well-behaved dog when he came home from the hospital. So I hung around whenever I knew Titus was due to take Kingsley for a walk."

"Which is why I had the feeling I was being watched," said Titus.

"Did you really?" asked George. "I hope I didn't scare you, Titus. I didn't mean to."

"No," said Titus. "I wasn't scared. But it was still weird. Then after we came out of the bakery I noticed the feeling was gone. That's because you weren't watching anymore. You had Kingsley back."

George nodded. "Yes, that's exactly how it was. I figured one of these days you'd stop at a store and leave Kingsley outside. And that happened today."

Titus was quiet for a minute. He was trying to remember something he'd heard his father say once. It was when his dad was having a polite argument with someone on the phone. Titus remembered what it was and said it to George. "George, 'you put me in an awkward position.' I mean, *I* could have gotten blamed for what *you* did. Sam would have known right away that wonderful little Gubbio wasn't Kingsley. Sam might have thought I lost Kingsley—and then tried to fool him by putting another Yorkshire terrier in Kingsley's place."

George looked at Titus in alarm. "Oh, I'm so sorry! I never even thought of that! I was just so desperate to get Kingsley back! Please forgive me, Titus. Peace?"

"I forgive you," said Titus. "But things still aren't very peaceful. Sam is going to be pretty mad at you for taking Kingsley. He's still going to want him back. And Sam is even going to be mad at me for not watching Kingsley closely enough. So *now* what do we do?"

12

Peacemaking

"*I*'ll tell you one thing," said Marie. "That Kingsley—he's not staying here."

"What!" cried George.

"No, I mean it," said Marie. "I'm putting my foot down. It's one thing to have a good dog around—" She pointed at Gubbio. "But that other one! That Kingsley—he drives me crazy. Besides, all this talk about pets has made me lonely for a cat. I want to get a cat."

Titus spoke up quickly. "There *is* one way George could keep Kingsley."

They all looked at him, waiting.

"He could move back home with Sam," Titus said.

"That old coot!" snorted George.

"But he needs you," said Titus. "He would probably never admit it. But he does need you.

45

Especially now when he's coming home from the hospital. For one thing, he needs you to help take care of Kingsley."

"Well," said George, weakening. "I suppose you've got a point there."

"Why don't you call him?" asked Titus.

When George didn't answer, Titus said, "Would it be OK if I called him for you?"

"I guess I can't stop you," said George. But he didn't sound at all as if he wanted to stop Titus from calling.

The phone was in the kitchen. Titus went

off to call Sam. Gubbio trotted along at his heels.

Through the kitchen window Titus could see Kingsley busily digging holes in the yard. Marie would love that.

The hospital number was already jotted down on Marie's pad on the wall.

"How's Kingsley?" was the first thing Sam asked.

"He's fine," replied Titus. "He misses you." He paused. "George misses you, too."

"That old coot!" snorted Sam.

"I think George would like to come home," said Titus carefully.

"Huh!" said Sam. "Did he say so?"

"Not exactly. He would probably never admit he's homesick. But he did wonder who would be there to help you when you got home from the hospital. Who's going to help you take care of Kingsley?"

"Well," said Sam, weakening. "I suppose you've got a point there."

Titus made himself sound casual. "I'm calling from Marie's house. I think George would like to talk to you."

"Oh, all right," muttered Sam.

"Hold on," said Titus. "Don't hang up."

He and Gubbio dashed to the living room door. Then Titus remembered to slow down and sound casual.

"George, Sam wants to talk to you."

"He *does?*"

"He's on the line now—waiting for you."

"Go!" Marie said to George. "Go make peace with your brother."

When George came back a little later, he was smiling.

"It's all set," he told them. "I'm going to move back home today."

"And you can take that Kingsley with you," said Marie.

"Oh, yes," said George happily. "Kingsley and I are going home to stay."

This was wonderful news.

But suddenly Titus had an awful thought.

Kingsley would never let another dog live in his apartment. And Marie really wanted a cat. So where did that leave Gubbio? Where was Gubbio going to live?

He put the question to George and Marie, Timothy and Sarah-Jane. But no one had an answer. His cousins sat up straight, though,

48

their eyes sparkling with excitement.

"Marie," said Titus. "Can I use your phone again?"

The rule was if something came up, he had to call home. Well, something had certainly come up. And to Titus, this felt like the most important phone call of his life.

13

Gubbio

Sarah-Jane and Timothy went with Titus into the kitchen, guessing what he was going to do. And, of course, Gubbio trotted along.

Titus took a deep breath and dialed his own number.

It took a while—quite a while—to explain that the nice Kingsley his parents had liked so much wasn't Kingsley at all but rather a wonderful dog named Gubbio who had no place to live.

"So—" said Titus, hardly daring to breathe, "Can I keep him?"

When he heard the answer, he burst into his own little doggy dance of joy.

George and Marie were delighted to hear that Gubbio would have a home with Titus.

George said, "I'll write to my friends and

tell them the good news. I have Kingsley back. And Gubbio has the perfect new owner—someone who's *very* good with dogs."

"And very good at figuring things out," said Marie. "All of you—such smart children!"

Timothy grinned. "It's all in a day's work for the T.C.D.C."

"What's a 'teesy-deesy'?" asked George and Marie together.

"It's letters," explained Sarah-Jane. "Capital T. Capital C. Capital D. Capital C. It stands for the Three Cousins Detective Club."

"Well, the T.C.D.C. certainly figured everything out," said George.

"There's just one more thing I need to know," replied Titus. "Where in the world did your friends get the name Gubbio?"

14

Saint Francis and the Wolf

George laughed and repeated the question: "Where in the world did my friends get the name Gubbio? You asked that question the right way, Titus. That's because Gubbio is a *place.* Gubbio is a town in the country of Italy. Something special once happened there hundreds of years ago. And even now when people think of Gubbio, they think of peace and friendship between animals and people. My friends told me their Yorkie was such a peaceful, friendly little dog that the name just seemed to fit him."

"What special thing happened at Gubbio?" asked Timothy.

"Ah," said George. "That was where Saint Francis met the wolf."

Titus sat up straight. "Like on the Saint

Francis fountain by our building!"

"Exactly," said George.

Marie got up and took a drawing off the wall. "Here is a picture of Saint Francis and the wolf of Gubbio," she said.

The cousins clustered round to see. The picture showed a gentle-faced man in a long brown robe. Next to him sat a huge, dark wolf. He looked like the big, bad wolf from fairy tales. But the look on his face was positively sweet. And, most amazing of all, he rested one of his paws in the man's hand.

"Once there was a fierce and hungry wolf," George began. "He attacked the animals of Gubbio—the livestock and pets—and even some of the people. The townspeople were terrified.

"Saint Francis came from the town of Assisi to help them. The people were glad to see him. But they didn't think anyone could help. They begged Saint Francis not to go outside the town for fear of the wolf. But Saint Francis was not afraid. He went out of the town to find the wolf.

" 'Brother Wolf,' called Saint Francis, 'Come out here to me.'

"Suddenly the wolf came rushing out of his lair, fierce and hungry.

"But Saint Francis said, 'Brother Wolf, I must talk to you in the name of the Lord.'

"When the wolf heard that, he lay down at the man's feet like a big, gentle dog.

" 'Brother Wolf,' said Saint Francis. 'I have heard bad things about you. You make war with your fellow creatures—the animals and people of Gubbio. This must stop.'

"The wolf hung his head. Saint Francis understood why the wolf had been attacking the town. It was because he was too old and frail to hunt with the pack. And the wolf was hungry.

"So Saint Francis said, 'Come with me, Brother Wolf, and I will make a bargain with you and the people.'

"The townspeople were amazed that the wolf hadn't eaten Saint Francis right on the spot. But they were even *more* amazed—not to mention alarmed—when Saint Francis led the wolf right into the town square.

" 'Good people,' said Saint Francis. 'If you will promise to feed the wolf and care for him, there can be peace in Gubbio. The wolf will not attack you. Will you agree to do this?'

"And the people all agreed that they would.

"Then Saint Francis turned to the wolf in front of all the people. He said, 'Brother Wolf, if you will promise not to attack the people and animals, there can be peace in Gubbio. The people will feed you. Will you agree to this?'

"Of course, the wolf couldn't speak as the townspeople had. But he could make a sign of his promise. He lifted his paw and laid it peacefully in the hand of Saint Francis.

"So the townspeople took turns feeding the wolf, and he lived among them as everyone's pet until two years later when he died of old age. And everyone missed him, for they had come to love their Brother Wolf."

"EXcellent story!" said Titus.

"Neat-O," agreed Timothy.

"So cool," murmured Sarah-Jane, sniffing a little.

"And I love this picture," added Titus.

"It's yours," said Marie.

"Oh, no, I couldn't . . ." Titus began, thinking that was the polite thing to say. But he couldn't help adding, "*Really?* Really can I have it?"

Marie smiled. "I *insist* that you have it!"

"Then, thank you so much!" said Titus.

"It's a picture of peace," said Marie. "Today you have brought peace to my brothers. And because Kingsley is going home, you have brought peace to my house."

Titus didn't say what he was thinking—that he hoped Kingsley would be long gone before Marie saw her backyard. . . .

15

Home

*T*itus was always glad to have his cousins with him. But he was especially glad now, when there was so much to carry. For a little dog, Gubbio sure had a lot of stuff. So did Kingsley, for that matter. George said he would stop by Titus's apartment later to get Kingsley's things.

Sarah-Jane gathered up Gubbio's toys and put them in his bed. She carried that.

Timothy collected Gubbio's dog food and dishes and put them in a grocery bag. He carried that.

Titus had the best job of all. He put Gubbio's real collar on him. (George had to get it off Kingsley first.) Then he snapped on the leash. With his picture of Saint Francis and the wolf in one hand, and his dog's leash in the

other, Titus was ready to go home.

When they came to the courtyard, all four of them stopped to look at the Saint Francis fountain.

Timothy read the words aloud: *"Lord, make me an instrument of Thy peace.* That's like what you were, Ti."

"I know what Tim means," said Sarah-Jane. "It's like Marie said. You brought peace. You were like the tool that put George and

Sam and Kingsley back together again."

"Oh," said Titus. "I never thought of it like that."

It was nice to hear. But he wasn't sure what else he should say.

It had been quite a day. Sometimes when the cousins had had a big day, they couldn't stop talking. But now as they rode the freight elevator to the nineteenth floor, they were all thinking.

They were thinking about Saint Francis and his Brother Wolf. They were thinking about peace. And joy.

And Titus's thoughts especially were filled with love. Love for his new . . . his very own . . . his just-the-right . . . *dog*!

The End